OMAR EPIC HERO

D1102623

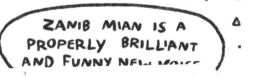

BIG-HEARTED, FUNNY AND VERY ENTERTAINING

THE BOOKSELLER

ZANIB MIAN IS A PROPERLY BRILLIANT AND FUNNY NEW VOICE

RUST

THE PLANET OMAR SERIES

ACCIDENTAL TROUBLE MAGNET

UNEXPECTED SUPER SPY

INCREDIBLE RESCUE MISSION

EPIC HERO FLOP

HODDER CHILDREN'S BOOKS

First published in Great Britain in 2021 by Hodder & Stoughton

1 3 5 7 9 10 8 6 4 2

A CIP catalogue record for this book
is available from the British Library.

ISBN 978 1 444 96098 3

Printed and bound in Great Britain by
Clays Ltd, Elcograf S.p.A

The paper and board used in this book
are made from wood from responsible sources.

Hodder Children's Books
An imprint of
Hachette Children's Group
Part of Hodder & Stoughton
Carmelite House
50 Victoria Embankment
London, EC4Y 0DZ

An Hachette UK Company
www.hachette.co.uk

www.hachettechildrens.co.uk

For all the children who remain their best

selves through life's ups and downs.

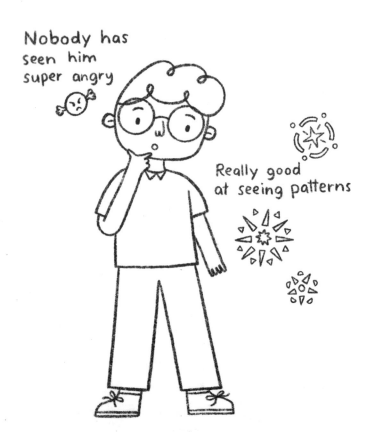

Mr McLEARY

Head teacher

Also known as McScary

Can be <u>super</u> unpredictable

Reads boring books

ELLIE

Perhaps a cheeky grandma in disguise?

SARAH

Can never tell what she is thinking

JAYDEN

Has great taste in pencils

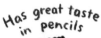

ADAM

Can hold his breath for a really long time

ROARR

CHAPTER 1

RRRRRR!

The sound broke through

the pin-drop silence of the classroom.

It was the sound that was the start of the

WORST TWO WEEKS OF MY LIFE.

We were having an IT lesson and my best

friend Daniel couldn't wait to show me the new

crazy video he had been talking about, of a lion

being friends with a human and saving her from an attack by a hyena. I had said he could just email me the link and I would watch it at home, because I knew that our IT teacher, Mr Philpot, would go absolutely bananas if he saw us.

But Daniel said, 'No way. I can't live through the WHOLE day without

showing you. It's only one minute long anyway.' And he hit the play button with the sort of look on his face that my little brother Esa has when he's farted

2

and he's waiting for everyone to smell it.

But it was the WOR$T idea possible, because:

- We are not allowed to watch videos in class.

- We forgot to plug in our earphones, so EVERYONE heard it.

- THE VOLUME WAS ON (((FULL BLAST))).

Ellie even screamed and jumped out of her seat before she figured out it was just a video. I guess she thought a real lion had somehow come through the door.

Our other best friend, Charlie, was staring at us from across the room where he was working with his partner, Adam.

HiS EYES TRiPLED iN SiZE.

Mr Philpot was scanning the few computers around us to make up his mind who to shout at.

You haven't met Mr Philpot before, so I will

tell you about him. Remember Mrs Crankshaw, the supply teacher we once had instead of our lovely usual teacher Mrs Hutchinson? The really mean one? Well ...

Mr Philpot made her look like a baby lamb wrapped in candyfloss with a drizzle of extra-nice sprinkles on top.

When Mr Philpot shouted, you could hear him from the other side of the school building. And even though he wasn't shouting at you, you would still shiver in your boots.

The good thing was, and this was also the only reason us kids dared come to school with

Mr Philpot there, was that it only happened every so often, not all the time. I guess some things really made him blow his top, and other things didn't so much. We hadn't figured out what they were yet, but Charlie was on it. Because Charlie likes maths so much, he sees patterns and common factors in everything, and he said, 'There must be a common factor in all the times Mr Philpot has exploded. We just have to figure out what it is so we

NEVER, EVER, like, EVERRRRRR do it.'

But with the video I thought we might have done it. I looked at Daniel and saw the horror in his eyes as Mr Philpot took big fat steps towards us. Daniel used to be a mega-bullying **TR⊗UBLEMAKER,** but those days are behind him. He hasn't been in trouble for a long, long time and I know how happy that makes him. But now he would end up back in the head teacher's office like he used to be ALL the time before we were friends.

I saw a tear trickle down his cheek as he put his hands on his ears to prepare for Mr Philpot's storm, and I knew I had to do something ...

CHAPTER 2

I looked at Mr Philpot, who was wearing his usual shorts with sandals. He had knobbly knees and something about them made me imagine him as an ogre covered in poisonous warts. This ogre was about to eat my friend.

I stood up really fast. My legs felt all

WOBBLY but I found the courage

to say,

'IT WAS ME!'

My hand went up to make super sure Mr

Philpot knew who to blame.

'You??' he said. He said it like he didn't

believe it.

'Yes, me, sir. I did it; you can shout at me in

my face, if you want.'

That made somebody at the back giggle, but

they quickly stopped when Mr Philpot turned

his poisonous warts towards them.

The whole class was looking at me.

That means around sixty eyeballs in total.

I could see Daniel from the corner of my

eye. His hands had moved from his ears to his

mouth, covering his shock at what I was doing.

Mr Philpot didn't shout. Instead he said,

'Can I see you outside, please?'

So I followed him as he

walked towards the door. I

turned round to look at Daniel, who

looked relieved, scared and super confused all

at the same time.

When we were outside the classroom

Mr Philpot said, 'Now, young man, what has got

into you? What a ridiculous fuss you've caused!

This isn't like you at all.'

'I know, sir. I'm sorry. It was sort

of an accident, I guess. I was trying

to catch my , which
had taken off into the air as if by magic and ...'
I babbled on, trying to imagine ways a video
could be played by accident.

   'OK. OK. Well, don't do it again, please,
Omar. You're a good kid.'

And that's it! I was let off the hook. No head teacher's office, no earth-shattering shouting, no anything at all.

I walked back in with a wide smile of relief, back to my seat next to Daniel, who could still be 'Daniel-the-kid-who-used-to-be-a-troublemaker-but-is-now-a-totally-awesome-well-behaved-kid' instead of 'Daniel-the-naughty-kid-who-has-gone-back-to-his-bad-ways'. That made me feel

really super fantastic.

I had helped my friend and everything had turned out great.

When it was time for break the first thing Charlie said to me was,

'Omar, YOU ARE a hero!'

Daniel said, 'I can't believe you took the blame for me! It was so crazy! I always knew you were cool, but I never thought I would ever have a friend that cared so much he would get in TROUBLE for me.'

OK, now I felt awkward and

shy because Daniel and Charlie were making it a big superhero deal. So I did a handstand to distract them. I had been practising at home and had only broken one lamp in my mission to get really good (and the telling-off I had from Dad was totally worth it).

It worked. Charlie and Daniel started clapping and trying to do their own **handstands,** which they weren't quite managing just yet.

Soon other kids from our class were coming up to me to ask what happened. And when they found out it wasn't really me who had played the lion video, but that I'd taken the blame so Daniel wouldn't get into trouble, they all looked at me as if I had burped a rainbow or something.

For the rest of

the day I got

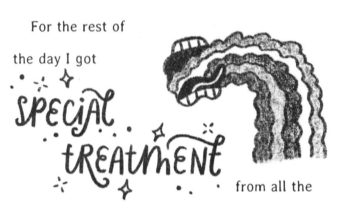

SPECIAL TREATMENT

from all the

kids in the class. The best things were:

- Sarah let me skip in front of her in the lunch queue.

- Jayden gave me his Pokémon pencil.

- And Adam even asked if I wanted to play football with him, which he has never done in the history of my feet stepping into this school.

CHAPTER 3

Back at home I didn't mention what had
happened at school to Maryam, my annoying
big sister, but because she knows me so well
she noticed something was different.

'What's up with you? Why are you taller or
happier or something weird like that?'

'I'm not,' I said. My secret was grinning
through my eyes, even though my lips
were straight.

'You probably answered some geeky

science question right at school and now you're showing off!' she said, walking off to show she didn't care anyway.

Maryam hates that I like science like my mum and dad, who are scientists, because she can't be bothered with it and always messes up on

SCIENCE SUNDAYS

– which is when our whole family does fun experiments at home in the kitchen.

I was putting all my school stuff away in the bedroom I share with my little brother when I heard wailing from down the corridor. Esa was clearly not in a good mood. He was doing that thing where he cries and talks at the same time, so it comes out all squeaky and high-pitched.

I went to see what he was on about this time, and it was because Mum had flushed the toilet when he was finished but HE had wanted to flush it.

'BRING BACK MY POOS!'

he was crying. 'I wanted to flush them! Bring them back!'

Mum looked a bit tired. Maybe she needed

one of her energy balls. She makes them out of
dates and nuts, which is boring, so I imagine
that they have more fun ingredients in them
when I eat them, like the milk of a winged
horse and a drop of honey made by bees that
live underwater in a lake called

the Pool of Powerful Energy.

That makes me feel extra strong when
I've eaten one. Imagination makes everything
more exciting.

'Do you need an energy ball?' I asked Mum, who looked like she was trying very hard to calm Esa down by explaining that once the poos are gone they are gone.

'Yes, please!' she said.

So I went to get her one, and, as I put the hard brown ball on a plate, I tried NOT to think about how it sort of looked like a poo. Imagining food as poo is something I would get seriously told off for if Mum knew. So I thanked Allah she couldn't hear my thoughts, put the plate on Mum's favourite tray (it's pink and flowery) and took it upstairs.

Mum was so pleased with me she gave me a great big hug. 'Sometimes you do the exact right thing at the exact right moment, Omar. Thank you!'

At home so no hijab

I love Mum's hugs, even though I never let her hug me in front of my friends.

I did something nice for someone again, but it made ME feel just as good as it made Mum feel. That's funny, right?

I went back to my room to go and play with the R🌸B🌸T I had coded with Dad, when I saw something out of place. A pack of cards that was signed by an astronaut Dad met years ago at a science conference. He thought I'd like a present signed by an astronaut and the only thing he had in his pocket was a pack of cards. Don't ask why. Dad always has

strange things in his pockets,

things you'd never ever guess.

And now the cards were sitting by my robot.
So weird!

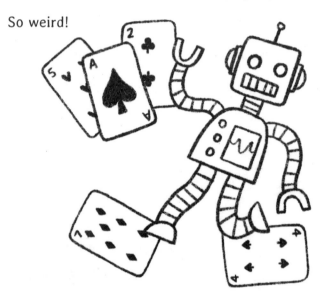

I was sure this was Maryam getting me back
for running down the stairs screaming the other
day, pretending there was a mouse in her room
just for fun. So I went straight to Maryam's
room and asked, 'Hey, Maryam, did you move
my cards?'

'No! Did you even see me go to your stinky room?!' she said.

'No ...' I said.

And she was right. I hadn't seen her anywhere near my room since we had got back from school.

SUPER WEIRD.

CHAPTER 4

The next day, as I walked to school, I wondered

if Mr Philpot had told Mrs Hutchinson about

the lion video. I know

that teachers gossip a

lot behind the doors

of the mysterious

staffroom, but I had

learned my lesson

about eavesdropping

on them from the time

I misheard some gossip and thought that my teacher had been taken by

ALIENS.

Anyway, I was really hoping he hadn't said anything, because I really like Mrs Hutchinson and I wouldn't want her to think I did anything **naughty.**

As I walked in, she smiled her usual smile at me and winked her usual wink, which made me think, **PHEW,** she doesn't know. But the most important clue of all was that her hair waved its usual hello. It wasn't her disappointed hair. I know exactly what her disappointed hair looks like, because I saw it last week when Ellie forgot to feed the class goldfish when it was her turn.

Charlie had his worried eyebrows on. They were reaching upwards and close together. I tapped them to make them go back to normal eyebrows but they wouldn't.

'What is it, Charlie? Who did it?' asked Daniel. Daniel still sometimes thinks that the reason for all problems happening is someone else being mean.

'Nobody did it ... It's my grandma.
She's really unwell,' said sad Charlie.

'Is she going to die?' asked Daniel.

I whacked him on the arm.

'What?' he said.

'you can't say things
like that...' I said.

But it was too late, because
Charlie was already sobbing, and hot tears
were trickling down his face.

Mrs Hutchinson was at his side in ~~a flash.~~
She took him outside to have a chat and we all
sat down to read our books, wondering what
she would be saying to him.

When Charlie came
back, his worried
eyebrows were gone, but his toothy

grin still wasn't anywhere to be seen. Daniel and I made our minds up to bring it back by lunchtime.

Our task for the morning was to think about mindfulness, and what we do to be mindful. And the reason was because a fancy team from a fancy TV studio were coming to make a news report about it and they were going to interview kids and teachers at our school.

'I've never been on TV before!' whispered Daniel, super excited. 'But I don't know what

 is.'

Mrs Hutchinson was asking the class what we thought it was. 'Hands up if you can tell me.'

Daniel shot his hand up, even though he had just told me a second ago he had no clue.

'It's when you make your mind full! Like, just think of as many things at the same time that you can; think about your sick grandma and your homework and why Ellie said your breath smells last Tuesday and how nice Mrs Hutchinson's hair is. Everything! Mind full.' He finally stopped, extra proud of himself.

I wasn't sure what mindfulness was, but I was sure it wasn't *that.*

Ellie and Sarah burst out laughing and started whispering to each other and laughing even more.

Daniel had turned jelly-bean red. And I could tell something terrible was going to erupt from his trembling lips, so I quickly said,

'THat's exactly wHat I tHouGHt as well.'

It was a lie, of course, but I thought it was a good lie because I could see he felt better straight away.

'Exactly! It's what it sounds like,' Daniel added.

Mrs Hutchinson said, 'Don't be so rude, girls.' Then she said to Daniel, 'Thank you for trying to make sense of the word, Daniel. I'm always very impressed that you're never afraid to try.'

Now Daniel **blushed** flamingo pink and completely forgot about Ellie and Sarah.

Mrs Hutchinson explained that mindfulness was actually the activity of noticing what is happening in the moment you are in now, to help you focus or feel better about something. It could be counting your breaths or watching how the wind rustles the leaves in the trees.

I wondered if she had done something to do with mindfulness with Charlie when she had talked to him outside.

For our task we had to think about what we already do to be mindful and plan what we would say if the camera crew chose to interview us. Mrs Hutchinson said she was sending

permission letters home for our parents, but

that the TV crew would only choose a few of us

to talk to, and it would help if we looked

neAt AND tiDY.

I tried to make my brain work super hard but

I couldn't think of anything I do that's mindful,

because I don't normally use the things in the

real world to calm down; I use my imagination

instead. (You might remember that sometimes

I conjure up my amazing dragon, H_2O when

there's a really bad situation going on ...)

Daniel spent most of the morning worrying

about whether he looked neat and tidy enough

or not.

'Don't worry,' I said. 'We've still got a few days till they come.'

As we walked out into the playground at lunchtime, there was a loud ambulance siren screaming in the streets. That was normal and happened all the time, but today it sent Charlie into a complete and utter breath-stopping panic.

CHAPTER 5

'What if it's for my nan?!' Charlie said each word like it was stuck in his mouth. His hands were shaking.

POOR CHARLIE.

Daniel and I both put our arms round him as we walked over to the school pond. It was Daniel's turn to test the pH levels of the water and it was mine next week.

'It's not for her,' said Daniel.

'How do you *know*?' said Charlie.

'Charlie, think like you do for maths. What are the chances it's for her?' I said.

But that didn't help, because Charlie started crying. 'The chances are

BIG—
they're HUGE—
because she's <u>so</u> sick.'

I felt so sad for Charlie that my own heart started hurting. It felt like there were tiny little trolls in my chest using it for a punching bag. And if I felt that, Charlie's heart must have felt like a thousand T-rexes were using it as a trampoline.

Other kids were starting to stare.

'Come on,' I said, 'let's go back to the classroom.'

We could help Charlie calm down in there and maybe Mrs Hutchinson could do some mindfulness with him.

'OK,' said Charlie.

He walked with us like he was some sort of

not really there.

'So much for making his toothy grin come

back,' Daniel whispered to me.

'It will come,' I said. I really hoped so because

I didn't want my friend to be sad for ever.

Ellie and Sarah were eating in the classroom and

Adam was showing them how long he could hold

his breath for. Mrs Hutchinson wasn't there.

'You're not supposed to

eat in here,' said Daniel.

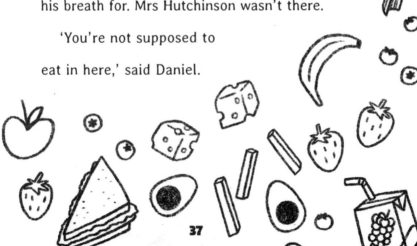

'So? What are you going to do? Are you going to *tell*?' said Ellie.

'If you do, we'll tell Mr Philpot who *really* played the lion video,' said Sarah.

Ouch. Sarah is really scary sometimes. Angelic on the outside and mean on the inside.

'What's wrong with Charlie anyway?' asked Ellie. 'Has he lost one of his freckles?'

'None of your business,' said Daniel, who wasn't happy about being threatened.

Charlie was at the window. Probably wondering if the ambulance had gone to his grandma's house.

Nothing I was saying was making him feel better. So I just stood next to him while Daniel tried to make the girls leave.

They were loving the chance to tease Daniel by not leaving and he was falling into their trap.

'Charlie! They're not leaving. Aren't you angry? Don't you want them to go?'

I knew Charlie did want them to go, but he never gets angry. Charlie has a few moods, but I've never seen him actually angry the way Daniel and I can get.

'All right, I'm going to try it for longer this time!' Adam was saying, but nobody was really paying attention.

The girls were walking extra s l o w l y to the door with their drinks in their hands. 'Oh no, I can't walk faster than this – I'm stuck in some goo,' Ellie said, balancing on one foot and laughing her head off.

But that wasn't as smart as she thought, because within seconds, her bright red Ribena was all over the floor.

'SEEEEEEE!' said Daniel as we all gathered round the puddle to stare.

'Get a mop!' Ellie screeched.

But it was too late, because just then our head teacher Mr McLeary walked into the room.

The six of us were frozen in our spots, all staring at our head teacher. Our head teacher was staring at the Ribena puddle. Nobody made a sound, except Adam who suddenly took in a big gasp of air. Would we all get in trouble? Or just Ellie? Would we have to say it was Ellie? Would she say it was her?

I looked at Ellie. She had never looked so scared before. I remembered how good it had felt when I had taken the blame for Daniel the day before, so, without wasting another second, I stepped forward.

'Sorry, sir. It was me. I know we aren't allowed to eat in here so I'm very sorry, and, erm ... I won't do it again.'

I heard Mum's voice in my head: *Sorry means you won't do it again.* (But does it? Because I have been really, super-duper sorry about things, but then done them again and been sorry again and tried not to do them again, but forgot.)

'Well, this is very **DISAPPOINTING**, Omar, and so unlike you,' Mr McLeary was saying through my daydream. 'Why did you think you could have a drink in your classroom?'

'He brought me upstairs to see Mrs Hutchinson because I was upset about my sick grandma,' piped up Charlie.

'Yes, because her chances are very big!' said

Daniel, which got confused looks from everyone.

'Oh ... I see. Oh, well, I'm very sorry. Hmm. It seems like you were taking good care of your friend, Omar. But stick to the rules next time, and get this cleaned up,' he said as he walked off, checking his watch.

'WOW! Omar, you got away with it again!' said Daniel.

'Thank you, Omar,' Ellie breathed, throwing her hands together and bouncing up and down. 'Thank you, thank you, thank you! You are *literally* a hero!'

'Like Spider-man!' said Sarah.

'We need to get him a T-shirt that says, "Super Omar"!' Charlie said, and FINALLY his

came back.

'Ah, it's nothing.' I sheepishly scratched the back of my head. But secretly I did feel super cool.

A very purple-looking Adam who everyone had forgotten about said, 'I held it for a minute this time ... Oh, never mind.' And then he walked out.

Mrs Hutchinson came back to the classroom after that, rubbing her tummy (she's having a baby soon, so she does that a lot) and looking tired. Straight away she told me that Mr McLeary had told her what had happened.

'It's a shame that the head teacher had to speak to me about one of my best students.' She sighed. Her hair was lifeless. 'And then there was yesterday, too.'

HUH? SHE DID KNOW ABOUT THAT?

I hung my head, and tried to imagine her hair singing and dancing.

She stood there for a second. I knew she felt sorry for me, so I looked up at her and tried to smile. She patted my head and said, 'It's OK. Chin up.'

But my chin was very heavy now, and all I wanted to do was stare at my shoes.

CHAPTER 6

I was going to use the weekend to think more

about so I would

know what I was talking about next week if the

TV crew spoke to me.

I was waiting for a nice calm moment to

ask Mum and Dad about it. Calm moments are

super rare in our family.

On Saturday we went on our usual trip to

the *Mosque* to pray, then we went

shopping for groceries and HALAL MEAT.

You can get halal meat in the supermarket usually too, but there isn't always very much choice so sometimes we go to the halal butcher instead.

 Dad waited outside in the car because the smell of the meat counter makes him gag, and while Mum was distracted, talking to the butcher, Esa took a bite of all the peaches in the fruit and vegetable display.

'For the love of bananas in pyjamas! What have you done?!' said Mum when she noticed.

'No nice ones,' said Esa. 'I wanted a nice one!' and he pointed at the peaches as if they had been naughty.

Maryam and I burst into giggles.

The man behind the counter was not laughing.

He was very cross. *Don't you feed your child at home?* he asked.

The silly question made the whole situation

funnier to me and Maryam, and we only

stopped laughing when Mum gave us a

deadly glare.

'Of course I feed him. It's not because

he's *hungry*,' said Mum. 'I'll pay for all

of these, don't worry.'

'I am worried,' said the funny man.

Mum handed him some cash and didn't even wait for the change. She gets **embarrassed** about things a hundred times more than other people. Knowing Mum, she will never go back to the same shop again.

Dad found the whole thing hilarious too. He laughed all the way home, which eventually made Mum laugh too.

We told Mrs Rogers, our next-door neighbour, when she popped over for tea, and she laughed till her eyes watered, and gave Esa a great big hug.

Maryam whispered to me that it wasn't fair that Esa got hugs and giggles when he was naughty. She thought he got away with too much. Usually I would have said something like,

'Right?! It's not fair!'

But I kept my mouth shut, because the last couple of days I had got away with things too. They were things *I* didn't **actually** do, but the teachers didn't know that.

We decided to play a game of Monopoly after we

gobbled up all the pakoras.

that Mum had made us for a snack. They're fried and that's probably why do they do extra-yummy things inside my mouth.

I passed Mum on the stairs on my way up to get the Monopoly and I slipped a bit, but luckily Mum caught me.

'Thanks, Mum.' I grinned.

'You're welcome. I'm just your friendly neighbourhood Batman.'

'Spider-man. I groaned. It's

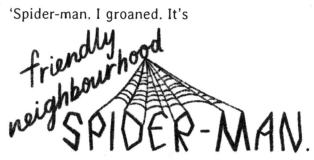

'Same thing!' she said. Even though she knew it definitely was not the same thing.

I shook my head at her the rest of the way to my room, and thought about how everyone at school was calling me a *hero* but also how disappointed Mrs Hutchinson was. It wasn't easy being your friendly neighbourhood anything.

I opened my wardrobe to get the Monopoly, and was super weirded out because the astronaut playing cards were now sitting on a pair of my folded jeans.

WHHAAᴬAᴬAᴬAT?

Who keeps moving these cards? And why?

I went straight to Maryam, the cards in my hand, and said, 'Maryam, stop it. You did it again. You moved these!'

'What's going on?' said Mrs Rogers, who was hanging out in her favourite armchair, watching over Esa while Mum and Dad prayed upstairs for the evening prayer.

'Maryam keeps moving these cards around my room and pretending it wasn't her,' I complained.

'I told you it wasn't me. You can ask Mrs Rogers; I haven't even been upstairs since we got back from shopping,' said Maryam, complete with and everything.

'She was right here,' said Mrs Rogers, nodding.

'Well, how are they moving to different spots in my room then?' I asked them.

'Beats me,' said Mrs Rogers. 'Maybe they are moving all by themselves.' And she gave me one of her confusing smiles.

The last thing I did before the end of the day was call Charlie to check how he was.

I was Super relieved to find out that the ambulance hadn't been for his nan, and that she was starting to feel better again. I could hear Charlie's toothy grin in his voice down the phone.

'You won't believe this, but the ambulance WAS for my street, though. Apparently some

kid got his

head stuck in the
TOILET!

Charlie started laughing uncontrollably, which

made me laugh too.

I think I was laughing even more because I

was happy my **friend was**

happy again.

CHAPTER 7

Sunday came round super fast, and I realised

that I had forgotten to ask my parents about

 because of how busy

Saturday had been.

As you'll probably remember, on Sundays we

have SCIENCE SUNDAYS

in our house. I was really looking forward to this

one, because we were going to be making

.

Goo is a pretty useless thing, if you think about it. But it's pretty useful for having hours of fun **Squidging** your fingers (and feet when Dad lets me) in a

STRANGE JELLY SUBSTANCE.

As I waited for Mum and Dad to finish what they were doing, I imagined all the things in a fantasy world that might be gooey:

- **Definitely a dragon's bogey (except H_2O, because he's special and so clean that his bogey is just soapy bubbles).**

- Trolls' babies. I imagined that they are actually born as goo and slide around across the floor until they're about one year old, when they start growing ugly troll features.

- Unicorn tears. Yep, I made unicorns yucky in my imagination and that's because I'm fed up of seeing them on everything in the shops. Once I went to a shop and I could have sworn my eyeballs had become unicorn-shaped just by seeing the things they were selling.

'Right!' announced Dad, holding up the dye we were going to use for the goo. 'Ten points for guessing if this is bogey green or mushy-pea green, but, be warned, whichever one you guess, you have to eat it for dinner tonight.'

'Don't encourage that kind of silliness,' Mum said, trying to hide her smile.

'Ah, you know you love it.' Dad winked.

'Bogey colour!' said Esa

'Ewwwww, you have to eat bogeys now,' pointed out Maryam.

'No! You!' said Esa, and didn't think twice about throwing a spoonful of yoghurt at her.

'DAAAAAAAAD! Look what he's done! I bet you're not even going to tell him off.'

'Esa, food is not for throwing,' said Dad. 'Say sorry to Maryam.'

'But I want to
do it again,'

said Esa. 'Sorry means never do it again, remember, Daddy?'

Dad couldn't help but chuckle.

'We can't laugh at all the naughty things he does, darling,' said Mum, swooping Esa off to talk to him in the other room.

I just wanted the fun to begin, but, as usual, there were too many

SHENVNIGANS

happening. Well, at least I hadn't guessed mushy-pea green ... If I had to have them for dinner, I would not be a happy Omar!

When we finally did the experiment, it was so much fun. Mum and Dad being the

CRAZY SCIENTISTS

they are had found out the chemical that toy makers put in that jelly powder you get to put in the bath. If you've ever seen it, you'll know that it's mad fun!

The amount of water in the tub grows and grows as it becomes this gooey jelly. The chemical that we used is something called

a polymer

that's 'pol-eeeeee' (like little kids say) and 'mer' – and it basically loves water, so it sucks

it up. Some
polymers hate water
so they don't suck it up at all, like
the stuff plastic cups are made of. That's why
they're made of it, obviously.

I couldn't help imagining different types of
polymers as little fluffy monsters who either
hate mushy peas so don't touch them, or
love mushy peas so gobble them all up. You
know which kind of monster I am. Charlie is

the complete opposite:
a gobbling one. I don't
know how he does it.

Later that Sunday we prayed together in
the house. Mum and Dad pray
five times a day –
at dawn,
midday,
afternoon, sunset
and night –

but us kids don't join in every single time, and
sometimes we just do it ourselves in our own
rooms. It's the same routine at home as in the
mosque, but instead of there being hundreds
of people, there's just Mum, Dad, me, Maryam
and Esa. Dad does the prayer by saying bits

of the **Qur'an** out loud and we all do the motions: hands on knees, hands and nose on the floor, then back up again with hands folded in front of us.

Esa always makes a mess of it, because he has no concentration span. Actually he does, but it lasts twelve seconds. After those twelve seconds, he either jumps on Dad's back when it's the nose-on-the-floor stage, or stands

under me when it's the hands-on-knees stage,

with his cheeky smile millimetres away from

my face or, worst of all,

The problem with all this is that is that we

aren't allowed to laugh in the prayer, and do

you know how hard it is not to laugh when

you know you're not allowed to laugh and

something funny happens?

It is HARD, and I don't always

manage. And if I burst into giggles during my

prayer, Mum and Dad get very angry, so I get

in trouble for something Esa did really.

Maryam struggles too, so we talked about what to do.

I suggested we lock Esa in the other room when we pray, but Maryam said that would be animal cruelty and then laughed a lot at her own joke. I said it wouldn't be cruel if he was happy in there, which he would be if we threw in some chocolates and toys.

Anyway, as you can see, Sunday was full of busyness too, so I completely forgot to ask about mindfulness and I only remembered when I walked through the school gates on Monday morning.

YIKES!

What if the camera crew chose me and I had no clue what to say?

CHAPTER 8

'Miss, when are the TV people coming?' I
asked, as soon as I saw Mrs Hutchinson.

She smiled. 'Well, good morning to you too.'

'Oh, sorry, good morning, miss!' I was
embarrassed. I had forgotten my manners, which
is something I never do with Mrs Hutchinson,
because she brings out all my *Pleases*
and **thank-yous**
and *excuse-mes.*
She even brings them out in Daniel.

She patted my head and said, 'They're coming tomorrow.'

PHEW. I was safe for now.

I gave Mrs H my best smile and decided to impress her with super-good behaviour because of her thinking I did two naughty things last week.

We poured into the classroom and I realised someone was missing.

'Where's Daniel?'

I asked Charlie.

'Don't know. Late maybe? Or sick?'

Awww, man, I hate it when one of us is sick and not in school. There always seems to be something we can't do because we're not a complete group.

But just then, Daniel walked in, his whole face red as a beetroot. I don't mean red like when he gets angry, I mean,

WHHAAᴬAᴬAᴬAᴬAT?

DiD YOU RUB BEETROOT JUiCE ON YOUr FACE?

kind of red.

The whole class gasped and whispered and looked at Daniel as if he had grown a mermaid's tail.

He slid into his seat next to me and opposite Charlie and said, 'Why do these things always happen to me? Huh? Can you tell me, guys?'

'Erm ... *what* things *happened* to you exactly?' said Charlie carefully, almost as if the red face would pop if he chose the wrong words.

I tried to imagine what would come out if it did pop. Red M&M's? Or something more like

gruesome

red zombie blood? Maybe Daniel had been bitten by a zombie so zombies were the things that had happened to him?

'I tried to look NEAT AND tiDY. for the cameras, didn't I?' said Daniel. He used his fingers to make air quotes so that Mrs Hutchinson's words 'neat and tidy' sounded like a mythical creature. Something people could never be.

'You tried to look neat and tidy by painting your face red ...?' I said, not stepping as carefully as Charlie.

'No! I used a stupid face wash, didn't I? My

mum's! And it made my stupid face red!'

'Oh, come on ... your face isn't stupid,' said Charlie kindly.

'Are you suuuure?' said Daniel. 'Not even *now*?' he pointed at his funny-looking face.

Charlie and I tried to exchange a look without Daniel seeing. Neither of us wanted to pop the zombie blood.

I tried to think of something helpful to say.

'Maryam had an ALLERGIC
REACTION

once, when she ate a tube of colourful sweets every day for fourteen days. But Mum gave her a tablet and it got better pretty much, very almost straight away.'

(Actually it still took at least twenty-four hours to get better but Daniel didn't need to know that.)

'Oh?'

My fib had worked. This 'oh' was hopeful.

'What's this magic tablet then? Can I have one?'

'Sure, I'll ask Mum,' I said. And then I got lost on my own planet for a bit. I couldn't help but imagine myself as George from Roald Dahl's book, mixing up a marvellous medicine for Daniel. I had always imagined the crazy things I would put in mine, but I never actually did it because my brother is truly silly enough that he'd take a sip when I wasn't looking, and I'm afraid it might do something a lot worse than make him grow.

After wisely giving Daniel some time to get over the fact that he had to walk into a classroom in front of thirty kids with a red face, Mrs Hutchinson came over to our table to talk to him. Of course she wanted to know what on Earth had happened to him and if he was OK.

'I'll be fine after I've had my magic tablet,' said Daniel. Which was funny and worrying at the same time, but I quickly explained to Mrs H what he meant.

We didn't focus much on our work that morning. Daniel continued to tell us how angry he was when he saw his face in the mirror. I tried to cheer him up by telling him and Charlie all about my SCIENCE SUNDAYS and how cool the jelly powder is when it turns everything to a big growing gooey mush.

'Wow, that sounds so cool,' said Daniel.

'I'm going to do it at home too,' said Charlie.

'Do it! All you need is the

It's really super easy. I could bring some in for you.'

The other kids in the class were only half focused on their work too, and very distracted by staring at Daniel and listening to what we were chatting about. Daniel's red face seemed to be the most interesting thing that had happened since Mr Philpot's shouting had shattered the fish tank. (We weren't totally sure whether it was the shouting that did it, or

whether some kid had knocked it over at exactly
the same time. I guess we'll never know.)

Mrs Hutchinson let us get away with being too
distracted to work because of Daniel's sensitive
situation, but she kept telling the others to stop
being nosey and get on with their task.

The nosiness didn't stop all day. It drove
Daniel absolutely nuts. We were followed
around the playground at lunchtime like the
royal family are followed by PAPARAZZI
(that's a fancy word for people who want to
take photos of famous people – usually to catch

them doing something

that would make great gossip).

Ellie and Sarah kept walking past

on purpose and giggling loudly.

Adam came up and tried to ask us

to play football again, but Daniel thought

he just wanted to be close enough

to see his red face, so he told him to

go away.

'I'M SO

ANNᴺGGGRYYY,

Daniel said, stomping his feet. 'It's not fair.'

Then suddenly, becoming aware of his own

stomping, he looked at Charlie's feet, which he

had never seen stomping before. 'What makes

you angry, Charlie?' he wondered out loud.

'I don't know,' said Charlie.

'Racism?' I tried. 'Plastic in the sea?'

'Yeah, of course. That makes everyone angry,' said Charlie.

'But that's not in just one moment. What makes you feet-stomping, eyeball-popping, table-smashing, car-thrashing *angry*?' said Daniel.

I LAUGHED. 'Nothing, because he's not the Incredible Hulk.'

Charlie laughed too. 'Yeah, nothing ever makes me *that* angry.'

Daniel turned round to see at least fifteen kids in their little crowds watching and pointing at him.

'Well, I'm bursting. I think I might turn green and big instead of red.'

He was sort of right, because by
the time we got in from lunchtime
Daniel was so angry he put his fist
into a nice ripe banana sitting on Mrs
Hutchinson's desk. You can imagine
what THAT looked like.

Mrs H came in, again looking like she hadn't
really rested during her lunchtime. Or
 maybe the baby in her tummy was
making her tired. The banana
was probably part of her lunch. She
looked super disappointed.

'Who did this?' she asked.

The class was silent. Daniel was squirming in his seat but not saying anything.

I had vowed to be good, but my best friend was already suffering a lot.

One last time won't hurt too much, I told myself.

And with a great lump in my throat I put my hand up.

CHAPTER 9

The teachers all thought I had turned into a

TR⊗UBLEMAKER.

I could imagine them having conversations in the staffroom.

Imaginary teacher 1: What's got into that Omar kid lately?

Imaginary teacher 2: He's behaving very unusually.

Imaginary teacher 3: Trouble magnet, if you ask me.

But with the kids I was a hero and they kept telling me so during after-school basketball club.

When I shot a hoop without missing, Jayden said, 'Cool guy! Cool hero guy!'

'Omar never actually misses,' said Ellie proudly, as if she was my grandma or something.

Adam hovered around me, even when I didn't need to pass him the ball. 'Is it cool being a hero?' he asked.

'Erm, I ... don't know,' I said awkwardly.

'I would take the blame for someone too, you know. If I had the chance,' he said.

'I know.' I smiled at him.

And then Daniel and Charlie randomly started chanting. 'Who's a hero? O-O-Omaaaaaar. Who's a hero? Omaaaaar!'

Daniel was so thankful he kept using his mum's phone that evening to send me messages on my mum's phone.

Daniel

Omar, thanks for doing the thing you did for me 😌 ••

He was trying to be secret in case either of our mums read over the messages later.

Me

It's cool.

Daniel

Oh, by the way, Mum knows what those magic tablets are but she can't give me one cos I have a bad reaction to them.

Me

What? Only you would have an allergic reaction to an anti-allergy tablet! 😆

Daniel

I know, right? It's not fair!

Me

See you at school tomorrow. Be sure to be 'neat and tidy'. He he he. 😄

Daniel

I'm not coming. There's no way I'm getting caught on camera with a red face.

Me

Awww, man! OK … Get well soon!

Daniel

Thanks. Gotta go.

This time I made sure I grabbed Mum

and asked her to tell me what we do at home

for mindfulness.

She thought for a bit and said, 'You know

when I tell you to look at the clouds, and for

a few minutes we just get lost looking

at how fluffy the clouds are and how

the wind is moving them and how

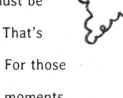

magnificent **Allah** must be

if simple clouds are so glorious. That's

For those

moments

everything

melts away and we are only thinking about

what's happening at that time to the thing

we are looking at. Using our eyes to be

aware of that moment. We can

also use our other senses to be even more mindful or we could notice what our breathing is doing or counting as it moves in and out of our lungs.'

'So basically it's forgetting everything else to really notice what you're doing right now?'

I said, trying to understand.

'Right! Perfect!' said Mum.

'Is it only when you stare at clouds and things?'

'No, no. It can be while doing anything if you get good at it.'

'Oh, so wait a minute ...' I thought. 'Are we supposed to do it when we're praying? Because Dad tells us to concentrate on the prayer and stop thinking about other stuff.'

'Yes, exactly.' Mum smiled. 'So if you could

manage to only think about you and Allah being there and melt everything else away, you wouldn't laugh at Esa's silly antics when you're praying!'

'Maybe I still would because what Esa's doing while we pray is in the *now*.'

'Oh yes, good point, SMARTY-PANTS, but if you really focus, you can tune out things in the now that you don't want to focus on.'

'How??'

'Just focus on your breathing and the words being recited.'

'Wow, cool. I'll practise when we pray tonight.'

So later, when Dad came home at the very minute when it was time for evening prayer and didn't even have time to take off his leather motorbike trousers before we prayed, I tried to focus on how the air was going in and out of my lungs, so I wouldn't think of anything else. Like why my astronaut cards were now sitting on my windowsill (they had moved again and Maryam had denied doing it again), or how I was supposed to look neater and tidier than normal for school tomorrow (though I think I'm pretty neat every day since Mum won't let me wear even my most favourite jeans if they have a 2-mm stain on them).

But, anyway, I was trying *not* to think of those things and only to listen to the words Dad was saying out loud from the Qur'an. I also had to not let my ears focus on the

Squeaky noises Dad's trousers were making every time

he had to kneel down. Luckily Esa was busy scribbling in his *How to Train Your Dragon* colouring book.

Mindfulness is really hard! But I think I managed to focus more than I normally do when we pray. *Maybe I'll get better if I practise every day*, I thought, as I went to grab a packet of crisps to take to my room.

Technically I'm not allowed to eat in my room, but if there was a chance they might pick me to speak to for the TV programme, I really needed to poke around in my wardrobe for my best Minecraft T-shirt while I ate them.

AHA! When I stepped into my room, I caught Maryam with her hand in my drawer!

And that's when we had a

BIG FAT
INCREDIBLY
GINORMOUS
FIGHT.

CHAPTER 10

Maryam has to be the most annoying big sister EVER. I knew that she was just pretending that she wasn't the one moving the cards around and then she wouldn't even admit it when she was caught.

'I'm just looking for ,' she said.

'You don't even let me *breathe* near *your* room!' I said.

Dad came in to ask what all the fuss was

about. I didn't bother telling him because
Mysterious Maryam would deny it to him too
and I couldn't be bothered.

But I stayed annoyed at her all evening and
all night in my sleep and I was *still* annoyed
when I woke up and ate my breakfast.

I stayed annoyed until I realised that if I
was going to be prepared for my day at school
with the TV crew around I had to find a way
to not let her bother me and figure out what
was going on with the cards later. I was also

worried about how Mrs Hutchinson would be feeling about me after the banana incident, which wasn't helping me to feel prepared either. I almost decided that I needed to imagine my dragon H_2O on the walk to school but then I realised I should just try to do the

magic instead! I looked up at the clouds to take my mind off my worries and only think about what was going on *right now*.

I was so busy looking at the clouds that I almost bumped into Charlie at the school gates. He was walking with a rigid robot walk and the strangest look on his face.

'Charlie?' I said.

'They're here.' Charlie tried to speak without moving his lips, and pointed at the camera crew in the playground with his eyes.

'What?' I laughed. 'We are allowed to walk and talk and be normal, aren't we?'

'Yes, but I'm really scared they will talk to me. So I'm trying not to attract attention to myself,' said Charlie.

'I'm scared too,' I said, only just realising how true that was.

'It's all right for you – you're a hero; you're brave,' said Charlie.

I giggled. 'I'm not actually very brave. I think I just made myself be for a minute and I was super scared!'

Luckily Mrs Hutchinson wasn't acting differently towards me. When we talked about the banana I had explained it was an accident: there was a killer spider in the classroom and I had tried everything to squish it, but it went and crawled on to her desk and I had squashed her banana while trying to put my fist down on the spider. I don't like lying and don't do it very much, and I worried that my huge imagination made my lies

too WACKY

but it seemed like maybe she had believed me.

I thought back to our conversation.

'So you go for killer spiders with your bare hands ...?' Mrs H had asked, one eyebrow reaching for the ceiling.

'Erm ... yeah. To save my friends.'

'And where is the spider now?'

'Dead. Super dead.'

'Well, thank goodness for that.'

What do you think? Did she buy it?

This morning Mrs Hutchinson's hair was not hiding the fact that she was really excited about our school being part of this important news report on TV. Her curls were extra bouncy and were acting as if they were dancing to a happy song.

She didn't make us work properly. Instead

she gave us a little drama lesson so we wouldn't be nervous about the TV crew. They'd be filming all day, all around the school, and although the teachers had chosen some kids to interview beforehand, the TV crew might also talk to any kid wearing a red sticker, which showed they had permission to be on TV.

Charlie was wearing a red sticker, but as we walked out into the playground for lunch he tore it off and looked at me with a face like the emoji who is very proud of what it's just done.

I half wanted to tear mine off, but I was one of the ones the teachers had chosen for them to interview and I couldn't let Mrs H down after all my attempts to be a hero.

I tried to act natural and went to visit the school pond for my duties.

I wish Daniel was here; he usually does this for me, I thought as I turned my nose away from the smelly pond while I checked the water.

I could have sworn one of the frogs stuck its tongue out at me, but maybe it was just eating a fly.

After that, Charlie and I walked around the playground with extra casualness until the TV crew came up to me with a big fluffy microphone and cameras the size of goats.

My legs were shaking and I didn't quite understand how they were still managing to hold me up as I stood there and talked about what mindfulness is to me. I tried to say about the clouds and the praying, but I don't know what I actually said. I don't even know if I spoke English.

I was glad it was over, and spent the afternoon lessons feeling like my normal self again, instead of my worry-filled self.

But it didn't last long, because Mr McLeary burst into the classroom and said,

'THE SCHOOL POND HAS TURNED INTO A HUMONGOUS PINK SLUSHY JELLY!!!'

And thirty kids, a teacher and a head teacher all turned to stare at ME!

CHAPTER 11

My heart was bouncing and beating so fast it felt like it was trying to escape out of my ribs.

All the faces stared at me with their minds made up.

OMAR DiD iT.

Omar *was talking non-stop about jelly powder science and* Omar *was on pond duty.*

Before I knew it, I found myself in a place I had only heard stories about from Daniel:

on the naughty chair in Mr McLeary's office,

squirming and wriggling while the head teacher

acted as if there was a really bad smell in his

room as he tapped my mum's phone number

into a thing called a

Landline.

It's called that

because it's a

phone stuck to

a piece of land.

In this case

the land of Mr

McScary's Room

for Wrongdoers.

But I wasn't a wrongdoer and I felt really, awfully sad listening to Mr McLeary telling my mum about a terrible thing that I DIDN'T DO, as if there was proof that I did it.

I couldn't hear what Mum was saying but she was obviously surprised.

'Well, he's been acting up lately and all the signs point to him without a shadow of a doubt,' said Mr McLeary.

He was going to make even Mum believe I had done it.

All my heroics to try to help my friends were epically flopping in my face.

I was trying to think of what to do and what to say.

I couldn't tell the teachers that I HADN'T played the video, I HADN'T spilled the Ribena and I HADN'T squashed

the banana. Because then everyone would think

of me as a snitch instead of a hero. If

I HADN'T done those things, I'd have to

tell the teachers who actually did them and I

wasn't going to do that.

Mr McLeary said that that Mum and Dad

were going to have to come into school to have

a chat with him as soon as they could.

After that, I did the walk of shame back into

the classroom and was surprised and really

happy to see a clear-faced Daniel. I

plopped

myself down on my table with my two best

friends, who seemed like the only two people who

didn't think I had put jelly powder into the pond.

'You came in!' I said. 'Your face looks better.'

'Yep, it feels fine now. Charlie told me everything ... This smells of duck poo, doesn't it?' said Daniel.

'Do you think someone is trying to frame you?' asked Charlie.

'Maybe. But it's not just me, all those poor pond creatures have lost their home! Who would do such a horrid thing?' I said.

'Horrid Henry?' suggested Daniel.

'Yeah, but the fact that he's
a pretend character kind
of made it hard for him.'
I smiled, even though my
heart was so sad.

'You're not the only person in the
world who knows how to use jelly powder,'
said Charlie. 'Why are they acting as if it was
definitely you?'

'Well, Mr McLeary said that it was pretty
obvious it was me, and he even asked Mum
what we did on SCIENCE SUNDAYS
and Mum had to say we used jelly powder.'

'Yikes. It does really sound like it was you,'
said Daniel. '*Was* it you?' he joked.

'⊗i!' I protested.

I kept looking over at Mrs Hutchinson and she wouldn't even look at me.

Daniel put his arm across my shoulders, and said, 'We're going to have to find who did it and stamp on their toes!'

'Or prove why I didn't do it.'

'You need an alibi,' said Charlie.

He was right: an alibi is what I needed. But it would be super tricky, because I *had* been at the pond around the time it happened.

I looked down at the table, trying to think hard, and that's when I noticed Daniel's white sleeves had pink stains on them!

CHAPTER 12

I felt like I couldn't breathe.

All the way home Mum was asking me what

had happened, and did I do it, and why did I do

all those other naughty things, and **what's**

got into me lately,

and was it the same reason I'd been fighting

with Maryam too?

But I couldn't listen to her properly. All I

could think about was whether it could have

been Daniel.

Maybe he couldn't
help being naughty,
maybe it was still
inside him like a
big growly monster,
trying to escape. Or
maybe he was jealous,
because everyone was
calling me a

hero.

He HAD come in late. He could have easily
done it without being noticed.

'NO!' I shook my thoughts out of my
head angrily. My best friend would
never do that to me in a million years.

'Excuse me, young man! How dare you say

no to me. You're already in a lot of trouble,'
Mum said.

'No, not you. Me. I was saying it to myself.
Sorry,' I told her.

'Well, that sounds silly,' she said.

'I know, but it's true.'

I hung my head. Everyone
was mad at me.

That evening we had a family
meeting. Even Mrs Rogers
joined in because she was
coming over to help Mum bake
cookies for people at work.

Dad was
TOTALLY
serious.

He's only serious about 4.5 times each year.

The last time he was this serious was when somebody had burgled Mrs Rogers' house while she was having dinner with us. He went straight out and got CCTV cameras to install at her place and ours.

'Tell us everything in your own words,' said Dad as we all sat round the dinner table.

I looked at Maryam's face. She seemed to be enjoying it a bit too much, probably because we hadn't made up since our fight.

I took a big gulp and started talking. I knew it was going to sound unbelievable ... FOUR things had happened. I didn't do the first three, but I had said I had, and I didn't do the fourth one and I never said I had.

Mum and Dad listened carefully while I talked.

Mrs Rogers got up for some water while I was babbling on, and a small but **Squeaky** fart escaped her as she stood up.

I carried on with my story, but watched my family's faces turn from serious expressions to embarrassed ones, losing focus on me, as they pretended not to notice.

'What's wrong with you all? It's just a fart; everyone does them!' said Mrs Rogers.

'I can't seem to hold mine in at this old age.'

Everyone let their relieved giggles loose and tried to focus on me again, but it had released some of the tension and Dad's face wasn't as serious as it had started off.

I looked at Mrs Rogers. She winked at me.

She had actually done it on *purpose*. I loved

her for that.

'So ... do you believe me?' I finished.

Maryam spoke first. I was scared of what

she'd say, but she said, 'Ribena. You never

drink Ribena; you say it tastes like

unicorn pee, so I believe you.'

(You might be

wondering how I

know what

unicorn

pee tastes like. I used my imagination.)

(And no, not everything I imagine is that yuck.)

'She's right. I believe you too, Omar. Taking the blame so your friends don't get in trouble is just like you,' Mum said, almost proudly.

'You shouldn't have done it, though. You should have helped them out some other way . . . ' said Dad, not quite wanting to let me off so easily. 'You wouldn't be in this mess if you hadn't lied all those times. Lies always come back to bite you; do you see that now?'

I did see ... because now I was in a big complicated messy mess.

CHAPTER 13

Walking into the head teacher's office with

your parents is the scariest thing possible.

Scarier than finding a spider on your

towel when you bring it to your face.

Scarier than farting in public

(which Mrs Hutchinson will tell you isn't so

scary after all).

Scarier even than speaking

to TV cameras.

And I was doing it that Wednesday morning.

Mum and Dad were sure they were going to convince Mr McLeary that their son was innocent. They believed I was innocent and they thought that two adults talking calmly to another adult would work magic.

But Mr McLeary is one of those people who when they have made up their mind nothing can change it.

'I understand that you're sure Omar didn't do this, because he's usually a good boy. A fantastic child actually. But kids change. I'm sorry, but I've been doing this job for fifteen years and I have seen perfect angels turn into fungus-filled tomatoes ... so unless you can show me some proof Omar is going to have all his lunchtimes in my office for a week.'

'Whatever happened to innocent until proven guilty?' said Dad.

'This isn't a courtroom,' said McScary.

And no matter what Mum and Dad said, he wouldn't change his mind.

WOOOAHHH.

A week of eating my lunches with McScary??!! I had to find proof I didn't do it, but I didn't know how I was going to do that.

I couldn't walk back to my classroom fast enough to talk to my friends and figure out an action plan. But on the way I couldn't help but think of Daniel's pink sleeves again.

As I walked through the door, Daniel was asking, 'What makes you angry, Charlie?'

It seemed like he was obsessed with this question. I guessed that maybe it's because Daniel isn't always the best at controlling his temper.

'I don't know ...'

Charlie was trying to concentrate on the maths he was supposed to be doing.

'I have to spend lunchtimes with Mr McScary for a week,' I announced with a lump in my throat as I sat down. I wasn't going to cry. Not in front of the whole class.

'But that's so unfair!' said Charlie.

'What? How can they make you do that? 'I'M SO ANGRY,' said Daniel. Then, with a flicker of hope, he added, 'Are you angry, Charlie?'

'Yes,' said Charlie. His eyebrows looked like they were trying to be angry, but didn't know how. He banged his fist on the table a few seconds too late for it to be believable, which made me giggle.

'We don't have to be angry, guys; we have to be smart and figure out a way to prove it wasn't me.'

I peeked at Daniel to see if he looked guilty at all, and I hated myself even more for being suspicious of my friend.

CHAPTER 14

We decided we were going to try to talk to other kids to see if they might have seen or heard something, or even know who actually turned the pond into pink, slushy, gooey jelly slime type stuff.

Golden Time gave us the perfect opportunity – it's the moment in the week when we are allowed to move around the class, sit where we want and do what we want, reading, drawing, making something ... **It's usually loads of FUN, but today we were on a MISSION.**

'Did you see Omar at lunchtime yesterday, like, not next to the pond?' Charlie asked Jayden, hoping someone would give me an alibi and say that I was somewhere away from the scene of the crime the whole time.

'I saw him in the playground, but I also saw him coming back from the path to the pond,' said Jayden.

He was right. I was at the pond. I even

touched the pond, but I didn't put jelly powder in it.

'Do you want me to lie, though? I could lie,' he said with an over-the-top wink.

'NO!' I said quickly. 'No more lies.'

Lies are like glue particles. The more you have, the stickier things get. I was already stuck enough.

Eight kids in the class said they saw me coming back from the pond. Five of those eight offered to lie since I had been a hero for other people.

Filip said he saw me in the school library for the whole hour of lunch. *What??? Ha ha ha.*

Adam said, 'Maybe it won't be too bad with McScary?' Which was stupid because it was obviously going to be the worst thing ever.

Ellie and Sarah said they actually saw me pour the jelly powder into the pond very clearly with their own two eyes. And then they said that even heroes get into trouble in the best movies.

'Yes, and then one of the lying baddies gets eaten by the monster!' said Daniel.

'I can't believe they would lie like that!' I said, walking back to our table and resting my head on it.

'What would Sherlock Holmes do, if finding an alibi didn't work?' said Charlie.

'Find out who bought jelly powder in the last few days?' I said.

'Impossible!' said Daniel. *Was he scared we would find out HE had bought some?*

shouted Charlie excitedly.

'Erm, random ...?' Daniel said.

'That's what makes me angry!'

'Soggy cornflakes?! Really?' I said.

'Yes, it makes me so angry when they go soggy **WHILE** I am eating them!' Charlie said, and sure enough he was turning red just with the thought of it.

'Oh, I like it,' said Daniel, grinning like the Joker. 'Bad soggy cornflakes. So yucky and soggy!'

'Yeah!' said Charlie, feeling proud that Daniel was so amused.

'Who would have thought? Out of all the things that make people angry, it would be soggy cornflakes.' Daniel was laughing so hard that the sip of water he was drinking went up his nose instead of down his food pipe.

'Ouch, ouch, it hurts.' He was scream-laughing.

I laughed so much the sides of my own body started hurting.

Daniel was just the best. I was being so stupid thinking for even a minute that he might have done it. I felt like such a bad friend. It was more likely that I would wake up with four legs than that my best friend was the reason I was in so much trouble. So I just blurted it out through my giggles:

'You know, Daniel, **I sort of thought you slushified the pond** because you had pink stains on your sleeves yesterday.'

Daniel stopped laughing faster than a calculator does maths. His face looked as white as a ghost all of a sudden, which was a funny difference from the colour it was just the day before.

'But I know it's not you!' I said quickly. I wished I had never said anything at all.

'It was Calpol, OK? I tried to give myself Calpol for my face and I couldn't open the bottle so it went on my sleeves,' Daniel said sadly, and he got up. 'I thought we were friends, Omar. I should have known it was too good to be actually and properly real.'

He walked away just as the bell went. I was left feeling like a right soggy cornflake as I made my way to Mr McLeary's office for my first lunchtime behaviour-fixing session.

CHAPTER 15

'It was awful!'

I found myself pouring my heart out to
Mrs Rogers at her kitchen table after school,
while she fed me all sorts of sugary goodies to
comfort me.

Mum says you shouldn't use food to make
yourself feel better, but it seemed to be doing
an all-right job, so I took another mouthful of
a triple-chocolate brownie and sprayed crumbs
on to Mrs Rogers' cardigan as I complained

about the mess I was in. 'And so, just like that, I was the biggest pond-wrecking, heart-breaking supervillain in school.'

Mrs Rogers seemed to find that funny.

'You're no SUPERVILLAIN, Omar, that's surer than the nose on my face. But you need to tell Daniel how sorry you are and how much you love being his friend.'

'I tried! But he wouldn't even talk to me after lunch. He was giving me the silent treatment, pretending he couldn't even see me, even when I did his favourite impression of a snake with legs.'

'Things always have a way of working themselves out, Omar. You've seen that happen many times. Like the time you and Daniel were lost on the Underground. That was terrible while it was happening, but it made you the best of friends in the end,' said Mrs Rogers the Wise.

She was right. I felt a lot better and more hopeful as I strolled the few steps back to my house. This was like the bigger-picture thing that Dad is always going on about. He says that even if something feels hard and horrible at the time, *Allah does it for a reason* because it all fits together to make something happen that is great for us in the end. Like a jigsaw puzzle that comes together to make a really nice picture. Even the bits of the puzzle that look ugly on their own are needed to make it whole.

I felt so good thinking about life as a jigsaw puzzle that I picked a flower from our front garden to give to Maryam.

'Thanks for helping me with the Ribena thing yesterday,' I said, feeling cheesier than ever as I launched the flower at her, imagining it for just a second as a rocket.

'Wow, you must really be suffering if you're acting this soppy,' said Maryam.

To my surprise she scooped me up in a big-sister hug, and, even more to my surprise, I started sobbing into her arm.

Mum and Dad were **very worried about me.**

It was super weird seeing them like that. Acting like boring, normal people instead of messing about and giggling and saying cheesy things to tease their kids. All they could talk about was how unfair it was, and how they couldn't just let it go, and how maybe they should talk to the

school governors.

I don't really understand what school governors do, but the way my parents were talking about them they seemed like mysterious creatures who control what's happening in a school. I imagined them all sitting round a table in a meeting room. They had long flowy white hair or big white beards down to the floor and curly black hats that had round pencils at their tips and wrote down all the rules.

'Omar shall be set free,' one of them was writing.

That night, although I had been feeling a bit better, when I was alone in my bed in the dark, the worries of what was happening came back. I tried to use my *mindfulness* to only think of what was happening to me right then. But my thoughts were too loud and my brain was flashing all the questions at me.

HOW LONG WOULD MUM AND DAD BE LIKE THIS?

WAS DANIEL GOING TO BE MY FRIEND AGAIN?

WOULD THE TEACHERS BELIEVE I HAD BEEN SO NAUGHTY FOR EVER?

OR WOULD WE FIND A WAY TO SHOW I HADN'T DONE IT?

BUT HOW?

CHAPTER 16

As I waited to see Daniel in class the next

day, I had a lump in my throat the size of the

mountain in Wales my parents

made us climb last summer.

I'm usually someone who

comes up with great plans,

but for this I had

nothing. I didn't

know what I would

say to him. I was

hoping just saying 'Be my friend.' would work, but maybe I would have to do something like in the movies, and pay someone to fly a hot-air balloon over the playground, with 'Be my friend, Daniel Green!' on its side.

I mentioned both these ideas to Charlie who said, 'Erm ... one's too much, and one is not enough. Maybe try something in the middle?'

Whatever I was going to do, I had to do it before I was sent to prison in McScary's room at lunchtime. But then Daniel walked in with a huge smile on his face.

WHHAA^AAAA^AT?

He sat down next to me and said,

'Be my friend.'

I was in complete hysterics at the joy of Daniel making things better and at the funny way he happened to say just what I was going to say to him. It's as if he was in my head. That's what makes us such good friends: we do and say a lot of stuff the same way.

'**PHEW**,' said Charlie. 'I couldn't sleep last night worrying about you two not being friends!'

'But I don't get it. I thought you'd be mad for ever!' I said to Daniel.

'Well, I was definitely planning to be! But I told my little sister Suzy all about what happened and she basically told me off like she was a little grandma!'

'Ha ha ha, why?'

'She hit me over the head with a stuffed unicorn and said, "You're such good friends! And he's only in this accidental trouble because of *you* and that video you played and the banana you squashed. And think of all the awesome things you've done with him and Charlie!" And

THEN she completely flipped and held my best

trainers over the toilet and said,

"How DARE YOU BE SO MEAN to OMAR? FORGIVE HIM OR THE trainers GET it!"

said Daniel, doing his best Suzy impression.

'Soggy trainers!' giggled Charlie.

I laughed. 'She's brilliant!'

'Yeah, I'm sorry, Omar,' said Daniel.

'Noooo, I'm sorry. I was being

such a brainless hamster,' I said.

And we did a sideways

sitting-down hug.

145

HA HA   HA

Mrs Hutchinson was telling the class that the

news report was going to be on TV on Sunday.

'I still don't understand what

mindfulness is,' whispered Daniel.

So Charlie and I explained everything we

had learned about it. I talked about trying to

focus on your breath and said that you could

count it going in and out of your lungs.

'Ohhhhhhhhhhhhh, right,' said Daniel.   HA

'Nope, I *still* don't understand!' Which

had our table in loud uncontrollable

laughing fits once again.   HA

Mrs H walked up to our table, 'Boys, are

you studying history or stand-up comedy over

here?' she joked.   HA

But she didn't give me her usual wink and

HA   special smile, which reminded me that   HI

HA

although things were good with Daniel again, my favourite teacher still thought I had turned into a **TR⊗UBLEMAKER.**

I finished my worksheet on medicine in the olden days in complete silence. I wished there was a pill I could give the whole world to make them see the truth. A truth-seeing pill, so no kid would ever have to go through what was happening to me. But then I wouldn't ever be able to tell kind lies, like when Maryam asks if she looks nice in her red strawberry lip gloss and I say, 'Yes.'

Before I knew it, it was lunchtime and I watched everyone run out of the door to the playground, while I carried my lunch to the head teacher's office.

'Don't worry, Omar. We're going to spend lunchtime figuring this out for you,' Daniel and Charlie had said before they went.

Mr McLeary opened the door to let me in and stood aside to let me walk past without a word.

Have you ever sat in a room with someone when neither of you is talking? It's super awkward. So I said, 'Nice shoes, sir.' Even though they were the second-ugliest pair of shoes I had ever seen.

'Oh, are they? Would they look nice filled with pink jelly?' replied McScary, looking unimpressed.

OK ... I thought. *I guess I'll have to sit in silence.*

I wasn't allowed to do anything except read. But I forgot my book so I had to borrow one from Mr McLeary, who was eating a sandwich I had seen a fly sit on seconds earlier. Somehow I didn't feel so bad about not telling him. He would tell me off if I did anyway.

I had read somewhere that flies lay their eggs on food, and their eggs are basically maggots. So when he choked a little on his food, and coughed, my imagination made me see maggots falling out of his mouth, which was super disgusting and made me not want to look at him any more.

The book was called *The History of Politics*, and it was actually more boring than sitting staring into space.

OH YEAH! All this chaos made me forget to find out how the astronaut cards were moving ... I was sure it was Maryam; I just had to work out how she had made them move when she had Mrs Rogers as her alibi. I would be a detective when I got home. I had a plan.

I spent the rest of the hour imagining what life would be like in space, which actually made the time fly by.

After lunch Charlie and Daniel spent the lessons winking at each other and putting their fingers to their mouths in a 'shhh' action.

'What's going on, guys?' I asked.

'Absolutely nothing,' they said.

'It doesn't seeeem like nothing,' I said, curious. Nothing seems like nothing when someone says it's absolutely nothing. But they just wouldn't say what it was. All they said was,

After today you're never going to have to worry again ...'

CHAPTER 17

When I got home, I grabbed an apple and went to my room to put my plan into action to find out once and for all how my astronaut cards were moving around.

Maryam had promised it wasn't her ...

And Dad had promised that ghosts didn't exist ...

My dragon H_2O was imaginary and only did things I made him do ...

I put the cards on my desk and crawled

under my bed and got ready to lie low
(literally) for a while ... Well, I didn't tell you
that it was a fantastic plan! But at least it
looked like there was nobody in my room.
And I'd be able to see who came in to move
the cards.

I took a bite of the apple.

CRUUUNCH!

Oops, too noisy. I was going to have to stay
very quiet for this to work. It was super boring,
but I stuck with it.

Finally I heard footsteps walking in very

slowly ... I pricked up my ears and opened my eyes wide, like a rabbit hiding from a fox.

I'd recognise the feet ... I waited for them to appear ... *Wait, what?* They were Mum's feet walking in. Was it *her*? But, no, it was a false alarm. She had just come in to hang a shirt in my wardrobe.

I waited some more.

Suddenly there was a very fast movement. Someone whizzed into my room so fast I didn't see the feet, and they whizzed around, jumping from place to place, making it super hard for my under-the-bed head to follow. It was ESA! And he ran out as fast as he had run in! He was like that little kid from the Incredibles. But why was he in such a hurry?

It was

his room too.

Surely HE wasn't moving

the cards? That seemed way

more planned than a three-year-old could

manage. How did he get so tricksy?

I quickly crawled out from under the bed to

check, and, sure enough, the cards were now

on my bookshelf.

That little ...

But Mum's yelling broke through my thoughts.

'OOOOMMMMMMAA AAARRRRRR! Come downstairs this minute!'

YIKES!

What was it? Mum only calls like that if I'm in

EPIC TROUBLE.

What had I done now?

'I just had a call from Mr McLeary.

Apparently, after school today, Jayden from

your class went to him to say that you were with

him the whole time during lunch on Tuesday, so

you couldn't have wrecked the pond. But when

Mr McLeary explained what would happen to

him if he was lying, he crumbled and confessed

on the spot that he WAS lying!'

WHHAAAAAAAT?

'Did you put him up to it, Omar? Because

that's what Mr McLeary thinks.'

'Of course I didn't! I said no more lies!'

And then it all made sense. That's why Charlie and Daniel had been so funny and said that I wouldn't have to worry again. They'd put Jayden up to it!

'Well, now Mr McLeary is really cross,' said Mum.

She kept talking but I could only hear her in the background through the fog of my own scary thoughts. My best friends had only been trying to help me, but this had made things a gazillion times worse than before. And things were TERRIBLE before!

'Oh, Allah, help me!' I whispered.

When I heard Dad's motorbike rumble outside just in time for dinner, I ran to the door. This was one of those moments when only one of his big strong hugs would do, and I wanted to catch him when he was still in his leather motoribike gear. Somehow the smell of it made me feel like everything would be OK.

'This looks really bad,' Dad said when Mum filled him in. 'If they were even slightly unsure

before about Omar being guilty, they will be dead sure now.'

'Yeah, only a guilty person sends a friend to lie for them,' said Maryam.

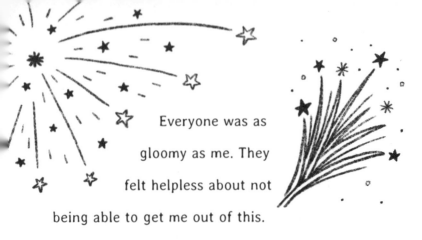

Everyone was as gloomy as me. They felt helpless about not being able to get me out of this.

'I'll go and talk to the head teacher again tomorrow,' said Dad, poking at his food and not eating it, exactly the same as me.

'I'll go with you. I think my son John went to school with Mr McLeary back in the day. Maybe some old memories will soften him up,' said Mrs Rogers.

I was desperate to see them all normal again. It would help me feel better too, so I took a sip of my fizzy lemonade and said, 'Hey, Dad, did you know that if you have a fizzy drink then burp and sneeze at the same time, it feels like there's a firework up your nose?' And I fake-smiled.

Dad fake-smiled back. I could tell because his eyes didn't go wrinkly, and I felt so sad at all this trouble that I thought I might throw up.

CHAPTER 18

That night as I was wondering if Mr McLeary would increase my punishment and how Mrs Hutchinson's hair would have flopped sadly over her shoulders when she heard about Jayden, Dad came into my room and sat on my bed.

'You know who's in control of everything, don't you?' he asked.

'Mr McLeary?'

'No.' Dad chuckled. *'Allah.*

He's in control of Mr McLeary and all of us and everything that happens. I just wanted to remind you to trust in Allah's plan, and ask Him for help, because he can show you the truth.'

'OK,' I said.

'Remember the jigsaw puzzle?'

'Yes, Dad. I have one of the ugly pieces right now.'

Dad laughed again. Yes! That was twice and his eyes had wrinkled too. I felt a bit better. He helped me pray to Allah before I slept, and tucked me in just like when I was little.

'I'll make a caterpillar in a cocoon out of

you!' he joked, wrapping
me in my duvet.

The next morning, as we left for school, Mum
said, 'Smile, Omar – trusting in Allah means you
don't need to worry about it any more.'

So I smiled at
her as best as I
could.

Dad and Mrs
Rogers couldn't
speak to Mr
McLeary because

he had gone to some head teachers' conference
in Oxford. But he had left instructions for what
should happen to me for the extra lying and
mischief he thought I had been up to.

Omar will have lunch in my office for a further week. In my absence he will have lunch with Mr Philpot and he may no longer sit next to anybody in the classroom until further notice.

YiKES!

First I had to sit alone and *then* I had to sit with Mr Philpot? Having lunch with Mr Philpot was worse than being stuck with McScary for an hour. What if I did something to make him blow his top?

Charlie and Daniel ran up to me in the playground as I was waving goodbye to Dad and Mrs Rogers. They felt super bad.

'I feel worse than Thor would feel if he had to wear a tutu,' said Daniel.

'Worse than a lactose-intolerant person covered in cream cheese,' said Charlie.

'Worse than someone who scratched a million-pound Lamborghini,' said Daniel.

'Worse than—'

'OK, guys, stop!' I said. 'You were trying to be helpful. I get it and I'm not mad.'

'Phew, thank you!' they said together.

'And don't worry about Mr Philpot,' said Charlie, 'I think I've figured out the formula. He always blows his top when these things happen together:

1. He is hungry. He's only ever blown his top before lunchtime.

2. Whatever naughty thing a kid did, when they weren't immediately sorry for it.'

And he scribbled on a piece of paper for me:

HUNGER x NAUGHTY KID WHO'S NOT SORRY

= TOP BLOWN

'Well, he'll be having his lunch when I'm

with him, so I think I'm OK ...'

I said, hoping it was true.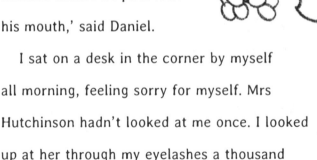

'Yeah, just don't even

breathe before he puts it in

his mouth,' said Daniel.

I sat on a desk in the corner by myself

all morning, feeling sorry for myself. Mrs

Hutchinson hadn't looked at me once. I looked

up at her through my eyelashes a thousand

times.

I wondered if I should just ask her if she hated me now. But I was sure she did and I didn't really want to know the answer because it was super definitely yes.

Sarah looked at me with a weird innocent but evil look on her face. I can't figure out *what* she is thinking half the time.

Charlie and Daniel waved at me a few times from their desk and I smiled back. And before the bell went for lunch Charlie held up his whiteboard with Mr Philpot's formula written on it to remind me.

HUNGER X NAUGHTY KID WHO'S NOT SORRY

= TOP BLOWN
GOOD LUCK!

Have you ever noticed that when you try to

do something extra carefully, you end up doing

the complete opposite?

I was trying to extra carefully knock on Mr

Philpot's door, not too hard and not so lightly

that he wouldn't hear me. Just the right

amount of sound, like the perfectly angelic

good kid that I needed to show him I was. But I

was trying so hard to get it right that I tripped

over my own foot and ended up slamming my whole body against the door. I froze with horrified scary horror eyes, thinking the worst, but, thank goodness, Mr Philpot opened the door with a mouthful of tuna pasta and I said sorry straight away.

Charlie's formula was correct and I somehow spent the hour with Mr Philpot and lived to tell the tale. I had done it. I got through the whole terrible day, even with a full hour with Mr Philpot. But I couldn't bear the thought that after the weekend I still had ANOTHER week of paying for something I didn't do.

CHAPTER 19

That weekend I tried to do the things I normally do, and enjoy them as much as I normally do, but I just couldn't.

I imagined what the newspapers would be writing about me if I was famous enough. I was certain I now knew how famous people felt when that happened.

I made a fake newspaper story to pass the time, drawing myself as a supervillain, with the headline:

Did you notice? Maro, my villain name, is Omar with the 'O' at the end instead of the beginning.

All of it made me feel a bit villainy inside for real. So I set Esa up for my plan to catch him properly by saying I was going to the garden to play but quietly sneaking back into my room and under my bed.

Sure enough, after a bit, Esa whizzed in.

I waited a few seconds for him to grab the astronaut cards in his little fingers before I pounced on him.

'Ha! Got you! Why have you been doing this, Esa?' I said, putting my arms round him so he couldn't run away.

'Esa's funny,' he said, grinning. 'Esa's very, very funny.'

I LAUGHED. 'Yes, Esa is funny.'

At that moment Maryam poked her head round the door and said, 'Bwa ha ha ha, he's my minion! The smartest pranksters always have help!'

'Ha ha ha, I knew it! You got me. I really believed you when Mrs Rogers said she was your alibi!' I said.

'That's because I wasn't lying. It wasn't actually me. I made Esa do it.'

'The pond thing wasn't actually me, but nobody believes me,' I said, hanging my head.

'That's because you're not as cute as me,' Maryam said, getting her strawberry lip gloss out of her pocket. 'Nice?' she asked, rubbing her lips together.

'Yes,' I said. And funnily enough she believed me.

Sunday was worse, because it was only one more sleep to school and SCIENCE SUNDAY reminded me of the jelly powder we had used last week.

I wondered what Allah was doing with His plan. He definitely always helps me when I'm in a mess but I couldn't figure out how He would help me this time. There was just no way of proving I didn't wreck the pond.

I kept whispering to Him:

I know you're there. I know you're going to help me. Dad said you don't ever need to take days off like we do.

Mrs Rogers came over to cheer me up and we played cards with Mum and Dad and planned to watch the news report on *mindfulness* that was filmed at our school.

Everyone packed themselves on to one sofa, super excited that they were going to see my little interview on TV.

When it started, we talked most of the way through, recognising different spots in the school and saying things like:

'Look! There's Mrs Hutchinson.'

'Oh my gosh, there's Charlie in the background. Why is he walking like a robot?'

We watched as Sarah proudly said her bit about how mindfulness had changed her life. And how Jayden said everyone should learn mindfulness like they learn to walk.

And when I came on everyone said,

'Shhhhhhhh. Shh. OK, SHHHH!'

And flapped their hands around to make sure everyone was quiet.

It turns out I did speak in English!

'I'm so proud of you, Omar,' said Mum.

And Dad messed up my hair to say the same without any words.

Mr McLeary was being interviewed next, and the camera moved to new a spot in the playground.

'Oh ... there's the pond in the background,' I noticed sadly.

But, as he spoke and we watched, we all saw something that made our jaws drop and changed the world as we knew it.

Clear as day, there was Adam, with five bags of jelly powder, pouring them quickly into the pond, looking around and running off!

CHAPTER 20

'HOORAY! THERE'S YOUR PROOF! This CHANGES everything! Thank You, Allah!' said Dad,

throwing me over his shoulders and parading

me around the room.

'Everyone in the school must have just

watched that happen!' said Mum.

'Those stinky puddles of vomit will be sorry

now,' said Maryam.

'I want ice cream!' said Esa.

'I want sweet potatoes,' said Mrs Rogers.

I didn't know what to say. It was crazy! I had been in so much trouble for what felt like months even though it had only been days, and the proof had just fallen out of the sky when I was least expecting it.

'Thank you, Allah,' I whispered.

Dad kept running around the house with me over his shoulders and I really, really laughed like I hadn't done for days.

Of course, the phone started ringing non-stop, as Charlie and Daniel, who had also seen what had happened on TV, wanted to talk about it.

On Monday morning I felt

really shy walking into the school. Although I couldn't wait to sit next to my friends and have a normal lunchtime in the playground.

Poor Adam. I wondered what would happen to him. He'd probably take my place in Mr McLeary's office at lunchtime.

I walked up to Mrs Hutchinson awkwardly in the line as we waited to go into school and said, 'Do you still hate me now?'

'Oh, Omar. Sweet child. No. No, no, I never hated you. How could I?' she said, her hair looking shocked at the question.

'To tell you the truth ... I mean, I'm not supposed to tell you the truth ... but since you're thinking something so upsetting, I must say something ... I never believed you did it. And I tried to tell Mr McLeary, but he didn't want to listen. I just had a **gut feeling** it wasn't you, and I couldn't even look at you because of how sad you were and how much I couldn't help.'

'Oh ...' I managed. My heart swelled like a balloon in my chest.

I wanted to hug her, but you're not really allowed to hug teachers, and all my classmates would think I was a big baby, so I just stood there while the balloon tried to force its way up my throat and into a hot relieved tear on my cheek.

Charlie and Daniel might as well have been holding signs that said:

Because they had the most excited energy
I've ever seen them with. Daniel took my hand
and waved it in the air for me like I had just
won a boxing match.

'Mr McLeary wants to see you in his office first thing, Omar,' said Mrs Hutchinson, smiling.

'Where's Adam?' said Daniel as we walked into the school building. 'He let you take the blame the whole time. I'll turn him into mashed broccoli.'

Adam was in the head teacher's office. Well, he was outside it, waiting to come in after Mr McLeary talked to me.

Mr McLeary had a strange look on his face, the way he might look if his trousers had fallen down while he was talking to the whole school in assembly.

'Omar, I've been thinking of what to say to you, but honestly I have no words. I'm ever so sorry for accusing you of something you didn't do. I'm very impressed at how much you care about your friends, and at how maturely you have taken this unfair punishment.'

'It's OK, sir,' I said.

'No, no, it's not OK. I basically called you a fungus-filled tomato.'

I giggled. 'You kind of did ...'

'Well, I'd like to call you something else instead,' he said, and pulled out a framed certificate from his drawer with my photo on it, which said:

BRILLIANT STUDENT AWARD.

But he didn't hand it to me. He said, 'I've called your parents in for assembly today and I'd like to give it to you then in front of the whole school.'

I beamed. I forgave him right there. He *was* really sorry.

Next he called Adam in to apologise to me.

'Why did you do it?' I asked.

'Well ... it was so cool that you were a hero. Nobody ever ignored you, and everyone wanted to give you stuff and hang out with you. So I kind of thought that maybe if I got you into trouble and then took the blame, then I could be a hero too.

AN EVEN BIGGER HERO.

At this point he grinned awkwardly and carried on. 'But then I lost my nerve. It was too scary. I didn't want to be in trouble the way you were. I'm not brave enough to have lunch in here ...' he said, looking at Mr McLeary out of the corners of his petrified eyes.

I felt kind of sorry him, so as we walked back to the classroom I smiled and said, 'You know he's less scary if you imagine maggots falling out of his mouth whenever he talks.'

The assembly was times a gazillion!

Mr McLeary and Mrs Hutchinson made a big show of giving me the Brilliant Student Award, which wasn't even a thing in our school until now.

They projected a very cheesy picture of me from when I was judging the talent contest on to the wall and played the theme song from a film called *Top Gun* from the olden days, which made Mum and Dad and Mrs Rogers go absolutely nuts and made me look like some kind of jet-plane-flying, world-saving hero.

YUCK! HA HA HA HA!

I looked round at everyone I loved, my family, my friends, my teachers. Even Mr Philpot was enjoying himself.

Who am I kidding? It was the most embarrassing super-best assembly of my life!

DISCOVER THE WHOLE PLANET OMAR SERIES!

ZANIB MIAN grew up in London and still lives there today. She was a science teacher for a few years after leaving university but, right from when she was a little girl, her passion was writing stories and poetry. She has released lots of picture books with the independent publisher Sweet Apple Publishers, but the Planet Omar series is the first time she's written for older readers.

KYAN CHENG is currently residing in Bristol with her husband and furbaby pup. One of her favourite things to do growing up was drawing characters from books and tv shows. She now has fun creating her own characters and continues to explore her favourite themes which include nature, food and all creatures great and small.